This paperback edition first published in 2014 by Andersen Press Ltd.,
20 Vauxhall Bridge Road, London SW1V 2SA.

First published in Great Britain in 2003 by by Andersen Press Ltd.

Printed and bound in China by Hung Hing.

10   9   8   7   6   5   4   3

British Library Cataloguing in Publication Data available.
ISBN 978 1 78344 017 7

This Little Princess

story belongs to

. . . .

A Little Princess Story

I Don't Want to Go to Bed!

Tony Ross

Andersen Press

"Why do I have to go to bed when I'm not tired,
and get up when I am?" said the Little Princess.

"I don't WANT to go to bed!" she said.

"Bed is good for you," said the Doctor,
taking her upstairs. "Sleep is even better."

But the Little Princess came straight down again.
"I DON'T WANT TO GO TO BED!" she said.

"I WANT A GLASS OF WATER!"

"There you are," said the Queen.
"Sleepy, sleepy tighty."

"DAAAAAD!"

"You don't want another glass of water?" said the King.
"No," said the Little Princess. "Gilbert does."

"Nighty, nighty," said the King. "Sleepy tighty, Gilbert."
"Don't go!" said the Little Princess. "There's a monster
in the wardrobe."

"There's no such thing as monsters, and there are none in the wardrobe," said the King, closing the bedroom door.

"Dad!" shouted the Little Princess.
"What is it now?" said the King. "You're not
still frightened of monsters?"

"Of course I'm not," said the Little Princess. "Gilbert is.
He says there's one under the bed."

"No there isn't," said the King, creeping out of the bedroom.
"There are no such things."

"Stop her!" shouted the Queen. "She's escaped."
"I DON'T WANT TO GO TO BED!" said the Little Princess.
"Why?" said the Queen.

"There's a spider over my bed . . .
. . . and it's got hairy legs."

"Daddy's got hairy legs, and he's nice," said the Queen.

At last the Little Princess went to bed.

Later, when the King went in to kiss her
goodnight, her bed was empty.

Everybody hunted high . . .

. . . and low, until . . .

"Here she is," said the Maid. "She's keeping Gilbert
and the cat safe from spiders and monsters."

The next morning, the Little Princess got up and
yawned a yawn. "I'm tired," she said . . .

"I want to go to bed."

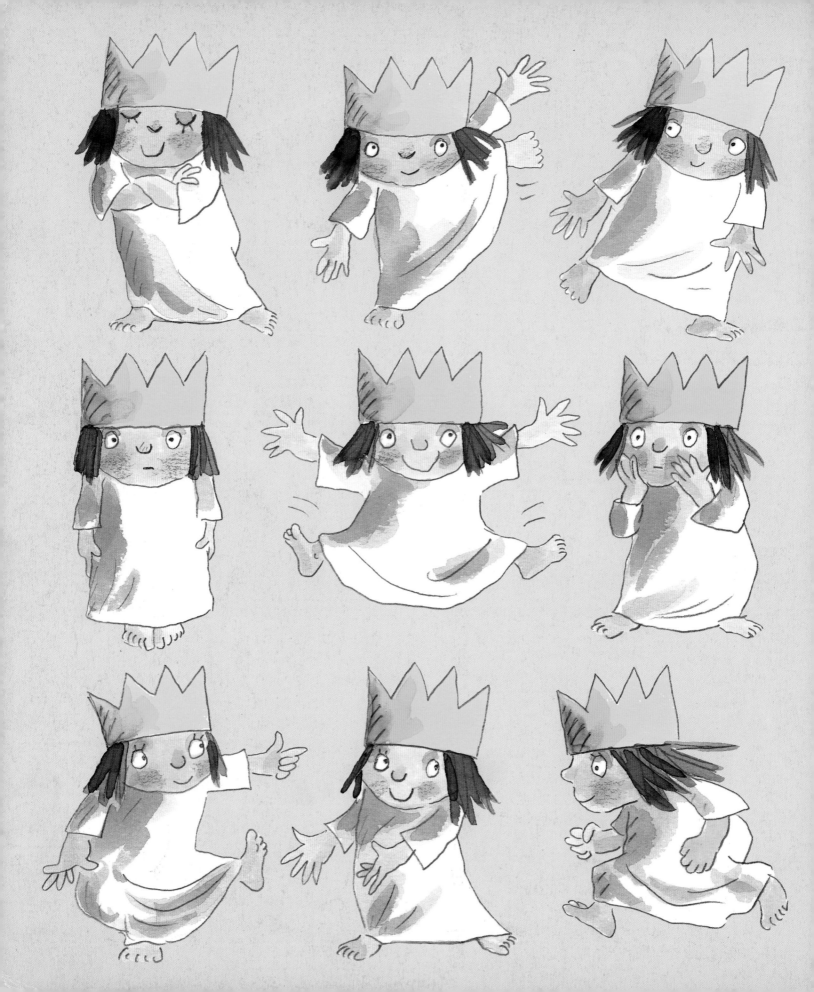

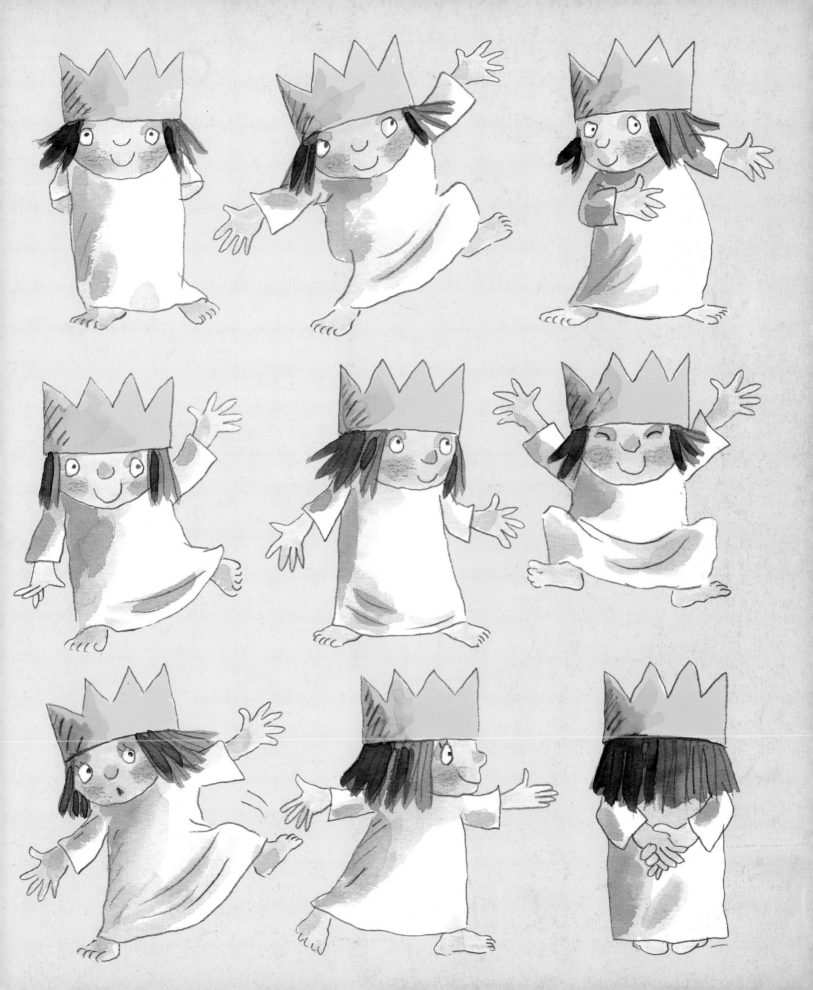